OK, Kids

by Bobby Lynn Maslen
pictures by John R. Maslen

Scholastic Inc.

New York • Toronto • London • Auckland • Sydney • Mexico City • New Delhi • Hong Kong • Buenos Aires

Available Bob Books®:

Ask for Bob Books at your local bookstore, or visit www.bobbooks.com.

No part of this publication may be reproduced, stored in a retrieval system, or transmitted in any form or by any means, electronic, mechanical, photocopying, recording, or otherwise, without written permission of the publisher. For information regarding permission, write to Scholastic Inc., Attention: Permissions Department, 557 Broadway, New York, NY 10012.

ISBN 0-439-14505-8

Copyright © 1999 by Bobby Lynn Maslen. All rights reserved. Published by Scholastic Inc. by arrangement with Bob Books ® Publications LLC. SCHOLASTIC and associated logos are trademarks and/or registered trademarks of Scholastic Inc. BOB BOOKS is a registered trademark of Bob Books Publications LLC.

6 5 4 3 2   10 11 12 13 14

Printed in China   68
This edition first printing, May 2006

Mom and Dad had ten kids.

Don, Dan, Jim, Tim, and Tom.
Pam, Peg, Nan, Jan, and Liz.

The ten kids
sat on Mom.

The ten kids ran.

The ten kids hit.

The ten kids did a jig.

The ten kids hid in a big bag.

But the bag had a rip.

Mom and Dad
saw the kids.

The kids got out of the bag.

"OK, kids, get to bed."

"OK, Mom. OK, Dad."

The End

List of 39 words in <u>OK, Kids</u>

Short Vowels

<u>Aa</u>	<u>Ee</u>	<u>Ii</u>	<u>Oo</u>	<u>Uu</u>	<u>sight</u>
and	bed	big	Don	but	a
bag	end	did	got		of
Dad	get	hid	Mom		OK
Dan	Peg	hit	on		out
had	ten	in	Tom		saw
Jan		jig			the
Nan		Jim			to
Pam		kids			
ran		Liz			
sat		rip			
		Tim			